Shapes

Written and devised by
David Bennett

Illustrated by
Tony Wells

Circle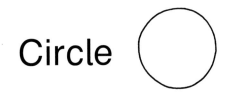

My wheels are circles
That go round and round.
They help me to race
On the bumpity ground.

What am I?

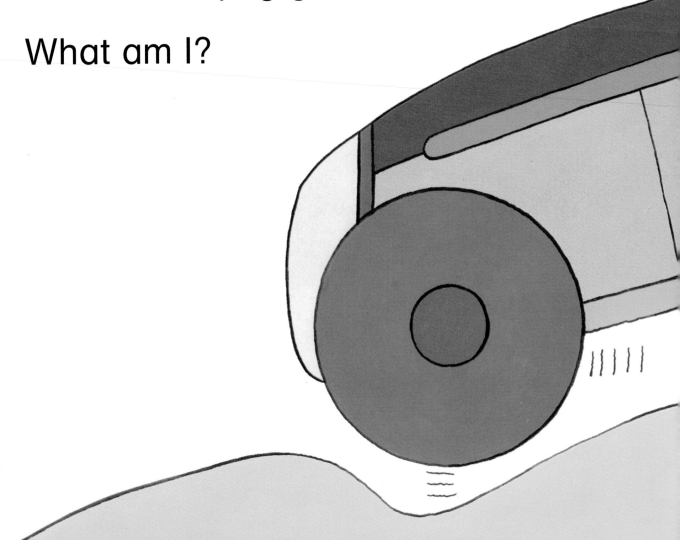

Shapes

First published in Great Britain 1989
by Octopus Publishing Group for
The Parent and Child Programme
Published 1997 by Mammoth
an imprint of Reed International Books Limited
Michelin House, 81 Fulham Road, London, SW3 6RB
and Auckland, Melbourne, Singapore and Toronto

10 9 8 7 6 5 4 3 2 1

Copyright © Reed International Books Limited 1989

0 7497 3018 8

A CIP catalogue record for this title
is available from the British Library

Produced by Mandarin Offset Ltd
Printed and bound in Hong Kong

Square

I am a square,
You can use me to play.
Just throw the dice
And then you're away.

What am I?

Oblong

My bricks are oblongs
That build into walls.
My door is an oblong
Where the postman calls.

What am I?

Triangle

My sail is a triangle,
With points one, two, three.
The wind blows me over
The deepest blue sea.

What am I?

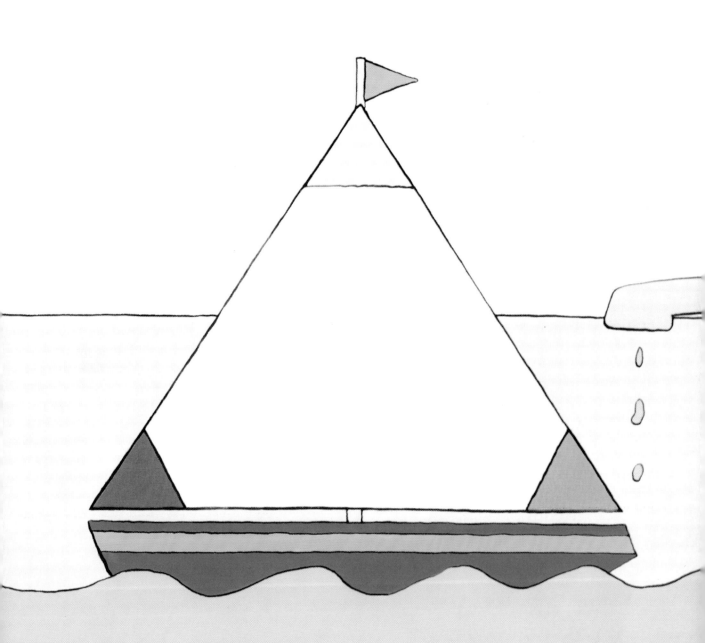

Diamond

I soar through the clouds,
High up in the sky.
My diamond shape
Helps me to fly.

What am I?

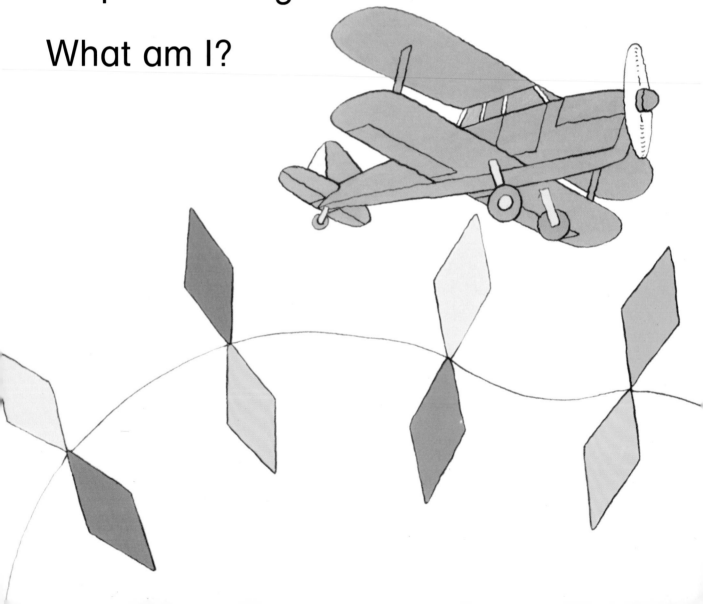

Star

I can sit on the top
Of a Christmas tree.
Cut shapes in the sand
To look just like me.

What am I?

Zigzags

I have got zigzags
Right down my back.
I breathe out hot fire
And my tongue is all black.

What am I?

Egg shape

I am shaped like an egg,
But I'm not in a cup.
If you fill me with air,
I go up, up, up!

What am I?

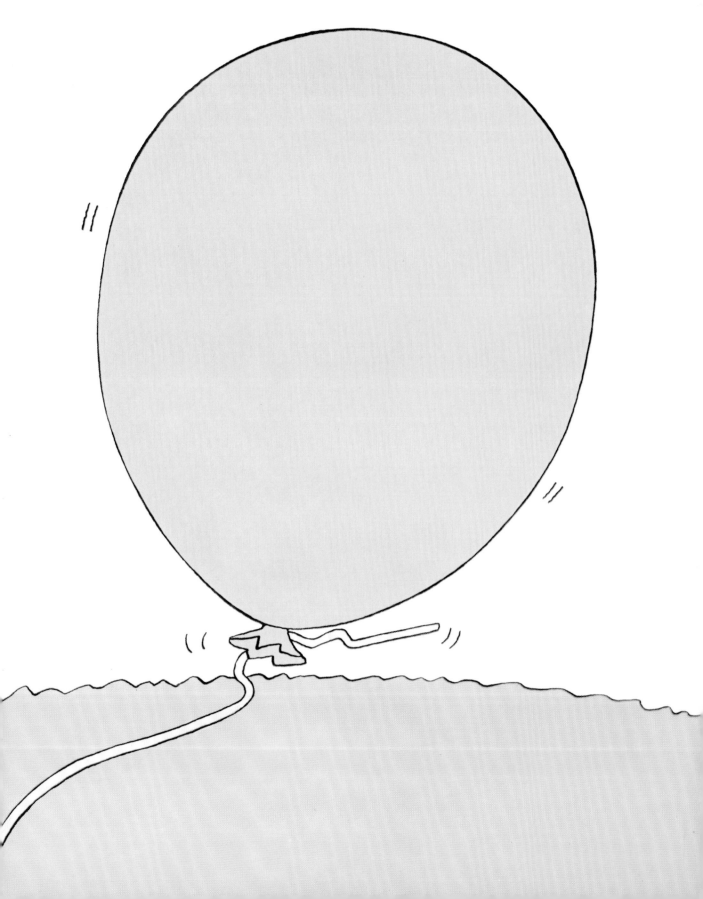

Wavy line

I'm just the right shape
For wriggling about.
I only say hisssss —
I never shout out.

What am I?

Now look at me,
I'm really the best.
I have the shapes
Of all of the rest.

What am I?

The Miseri
Holy Trinity

STRATFORD-UPON-AVON

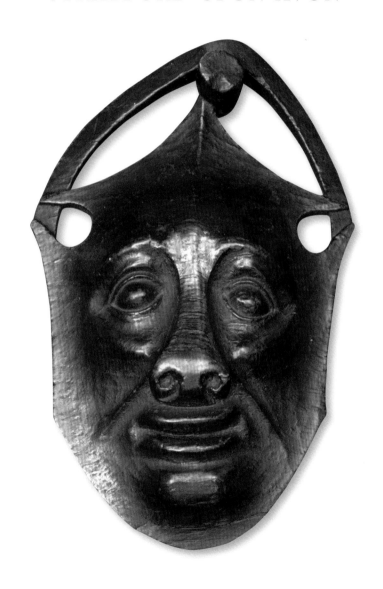

Researched and written by Madeleine Hammond *MSt (Oxon) English Local History*
Photographs by John Cheal *"Inspired Images"*

Holy Trinity church has a remarkable wealth of history and our misericords, with their intricate carvings, are a part of that journey through time. These wooden seats in the chancel offer a unique glimpse into the mediaeval world. Not only have they survived the destruction and upheaval of the Reformation and English civil war, but also centuries of use. This booklet offers some thoughts on their use and possible interpretations of the meanings of their elaborate carvings.

CONTENTS

Introduction 3

The 26 misericords of Holy Trinity Church 8

North side misericords 10

Wall-mounted misericords 18

South side misericords 20

Bench ends 30

Notes and Bibliography 32

ACKNOWLEDGEMENTS

With grateful thanks to Val Horsler and Clifford Manlow. By kind permission of the Vicar and churchwardens of Holy Trinity Church.

Designed by Clifford Manlow
Printed by Lexon Group
ISBN 978-0-9573142-1-4
Researched and written by Madeleine Hammond
Text copyright © Madeleine Hammond 2013
All photographs copyright © John Cheal "Inspired Images" 2013
First published 2013
A CJ HAMMOND PUBLICATION

Left: Woman's figure from misericord 1

Introduction

Holy Trinity was originally built in the shape of the Cross, with a nave and chancel. The nave was separated from the chancel by the great rood (Cross), with a statue of the crucified Christ. There were also statues of Mary and John on either side of Christ. From earliest times the nave was the place where the townspeople came to worship; the chancel was only used by the clergy. The people would stand and listen to the mass from the nave. Prior to the Reformation there were no seats in the nave for people; everybody had to stand[1].

In the 14th century, two chapels were added at the sides of the nave. The Lady (or Guild) Chapel was on the left-hand side. It was the founding of the chantry chapel dedicated to St Thomas Becket of Canterbury, on the right-hand side of the nave, that began Holy Trinity's collegiate story in 1331. Chantry chapels, which were abolished at the Reformation, were created specifically to say masses and pray for the souls of their benefactors.

John de Stratforde founded the chapel, which had a warden, a sub-warden and three priests. The chapel flourished and John (along with others) endowed the chantry with lands and eventually purchased the living of the church from the Bishop of Worcester[2]. By 1352 a house for the priests had been built by Ralph de Stratforde (his nephew), opposite the west end of the church. Henry V officially converted the chantry to a college by conferring its collegiate privileges in 1415. From that date Holy Trinity was known as The Collegiate Church of the Holy and Undivided Trinity, and the head of the college became a Dean (instead of Rector).

The priests of Holy Trinity's college were celibate and lived as a close-knit religious community but were not in training for the priesthood in closed orders, nor did they take vows of poverty or chastity. These priests were Augustinian canons, who were governed by the rules (or canons) of the church and answered to the Bishop of Worcester. They continued to have contact with the world outside the church. Their commitment was to sing the eight daily offices in the chancel of the church: Matins, Lauds, Prime, Terce, Sext, Nones, Vespers and Compline, as well as celebrating one or two high masses[3]. Later on four child choristers were also appointed by Ralph Collingwood (Dean from 1491 to 1578) to assist daily with the celebration of divine service[4].

It was Dean Thomas Balsall who completely rebuilt the chancel between 1466 and 1491, and installed the misericords.

Above: Leaf arrangement from misericord 6
Below: View of misericords on north side

WHO CARVED THE MISERICORDS?

The standard of carving on the majority of misericords, in Holy Trinity and other mediaeval churches across the country, is uniformly very high. The carvings were created from a single piece of wood by local skilled carpenters, usually members of a Craft Guild, who had learned their craft without schooling or textbooks. They often moved on from one job to another within the locality[6]. Misericord seats were not restricted solely to English monasteries and churches; they were also used in churches across Europe.

WHAT DO THE CARVINGS MEAN?

Misericords evolved in a world where the majority of people were unable to read or write. Churches were full of visual imagery with religious stories portrayed in wall paintings, stained glass windows and statues of saints. Every form of decoration was used to convey messages about good and evil, right and wrong, the stories of Christ and the saints.

There are no religious scenes depicted on the misericords in the chancel of Holy Trinity, although they are to be found in other churches. The carvings

THE PURPOSE OF MISERICORDS

The priests had to stand for all services, except for the Epistle and Gradual at Mass and the Response at Vespers. This was particularly hard on older or weaker priests[5] and so misericords evolved to help those who were not able to stand for long periods. Effectively, they were an early form of tip-up seat comprising a normal wooden hinged seat with a small ledge on its underside, big enough to support a person's weight.

An infirm or elderly priest could therefore rest on the small seat during services and yet appear to be standing. The extraordinary carvings are only visible when the seat is folded up. The name "misericord" is derived from the Latin word *miserere* meaning "mercy".

Above: View of misericords on south side
Right: View of misericords on north side
Top right: A small shield from misericord 25 showing three small crosses symbolising the Holy Trinity
Far right: Foliage from misericord 9 symbolising God's creation of life and nature

here depict, in the main, the same sorts of mythical animals and humans that also feature in illuminated psalters, manuscripts, mosaics and woven into tapestries of the mediaeval period, laden with allegorical meaning.

Misericord seats in churches and monasteries across the country were all carved to the same format, with three elements on each seat. The centrepiece carries the main theme, with additional carvings on each side called the left and right "supporters". Also in Holy Trinity, the armrests that separate the seats each display a beautifully carved angel (almost like a sentinel standing guard). There is one exception to the usual format in Holy Trinity's carved seats; on the south side, misericord 18 has three carvings of the face of one woman.

The carvings are a mixture of bawdy and satirical with a theatrical, almost carnival-like element, but with an underlying sacred meaning. They are a stark reminder that the devil is everywhere in everyday life and is poised to drag souls to hell. A constant theme underpinning misericord carvings across the country is that women *en masse* must be kept firmly in check and not allowed to get out of hand. The

sacred Virgin Mary is the only exception to this.

There is a theory that holy people or sacred scenes were not often carved because it would be sacrilegious to sit on them. On the other hand, when the seat was fully lowered, the occupant was sitting firmly on the temptations depicted in the carvings!

The clergy of the 15th century would have been able to read the images as a visual language. They may seem rather strange through today's eyes, but the moral teaching they portrayed would have been understood by people of that time[7]. The church authorities controlled the content of the carvings, in accordance with established religious conventions, but it was then left to the carvers to interpret the themes in their own way[8]. In essence, the basic message is the fight between good and evil.

Fortunately, at the time of the Reformation, the scenes carved on the misericords were not considered as offensive as the images in stained glass, wall paintings and statues. Given that many of these misericords have been subjected to defacing at some point, we are exceedingly lucky that so much carving has survived. It is estimated that 97% of all religious art was destroyed during the Reformation and Cromwell's purges[9].

THE MAIN THEMES OF THE CARVINGS AND THEIR AUDIENCE

There are three strong messages conveyed in these misericords: warnings against being seduced into sin (almost always caused by women); the result of being snatched into a sinful life by the devil in everyday life; and, as a contrast, celebration and rejoicing for those who lead a life within Christ's teachings.

Another constant thread that quietly interweaves its way through all these carvings (including those on the bench ends) is all the different varieties of trees, leaves and foliage. This is a celebration of God's creation of life in all its forms and that His love is always present, regardless of the sin that abounds everywhere.

There are almost certainly much deeper meanings within these carvings, which are not easily identified by modern eyes. For example, the Evangelists, Matthew, Mark, Luke and John, are often depicted in stained glass windows by the images of a man, a lion, an ox and an eagle. Here in Holy Trinity, there are four misericord carvings symbolising the Evangelists: two of Mark and Luke on the north side, and two of Matthew and John on the south side.

- Mark – a lion *(centrepiece of misericord 7, north side)*.
- Luke – an ox *(centrepiece of misericord 9, north side)*.
- Matthew – a man *(the right-hand supporter of misericord 16, south side)*.
- John – an eagle *(centrepiece of misericord 26, south side)*.

The symbolism of these carvings would have been recognised by the priests as a silent tribute to the four Evangelists.

In those pre-Reformation days, the chancel was closed to everyone except the clergy. They were the only people to see the carvings day-in-day-out on the misericord seats. The priests in collegiate churches were

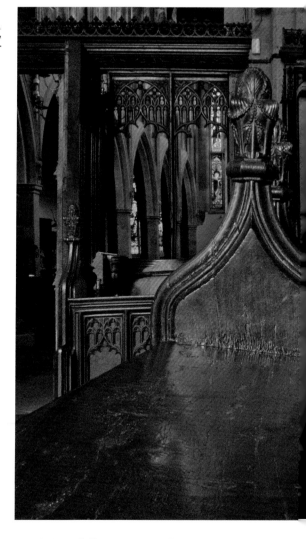

in a slightly different position from those in closed orders, since they continued to have contact with people in the world outside the church. Even though they were governed by the rules of the church, they were subjected to the same temptations as other men.

Above: A goat depicted in misericord 21 symbolising the damned

Above: A woman depicted in misericord 20 symbolising lechery and evil

Above: Vine leaves and grapes depicted in misericord 6 symbolising God's creation of life and nature

This strongly suggests that the warnings on the misericords were targeted specifically at the priests and clergy. They were being warned to stay away from women who could seduce men into sin. Women are portrayed as seductive, fierce or abusive, able to entice men onto the rock of sin, dominate or attack them, and always needed to be kept strictly under control. Other misericord carvings were also potent visual reminders of the devil in other guises lurking in everyday life as it was perceived in the 15th century. The carvings were almost certainly intended to give a strong framework of spiritual guidance to the priests and clergy, to help prevent them from straying from the path of celibacy[10] and as an aid to finding their own self-discipline and dignity. They were also perhaps designed to guide the priests' interaction and dealings with the people they met in the world outside, to keep them on the straight and narrow.

Misericords are a part of our national church history and in each cathedral, abbey or church that still has them, the carvings conform to the same pattern of centrepiece with left and right supporters. In different areas, though, misericords will often reflect aspects of their own locality (trades local to the area, or local patrons for example).

These misericords are a unique art form and a tribute to the artistry and skill of the wood carvers of that period. Inevitably, there will be aspects of the visual language of these carvings that are incomprehensible to our minds today, with deep, enigmatic meanings which will probably remain a closed book to modern eyes.

Above: View of misericords on north side
Left: Bench end (c) showing leaves (may be poppy leaves)

THE 26 MISERICORDS O

There are 26 misericords in the chancel: 13 on the north side and 13 on the south. (There are also two part-misericords which are wall-mounted on the north and south walls of the chancel. These were originally from the Thomas Becket Chapel[11]).

There is a marked difference between the subject matter of the misericord carvings on the north and south sides. Those on the north side depict stark warnings against men being seduced by women, that the devil is hidden everywhere waiting to snatch

HOLY TRINITY CHURCH

unsuspecting souls and the contrast of living in harmony and peace within Christ's teaching.

The carvings on the south side largely depict the fate of those who have yielded to sinful ways and the mayhem they suffer as a result. Women feature largely as being the root cause of disharmony and evil on both north and south sides. In absolute contrast, the crucifixion of Christ is depicted in misericord 25 (the capture of the unicorn) and the representation of God's creation is portrayed in foliage, leaves and trees.

Below: View of the chancel taken from the high altar

For the location of the numbered misericord images overleaf see chancel floor plan, inside front cover. 01 refers to the numbers on the chancel floor plan.

North side misericords

The centrepiece shows a man and woman rising from whelk shells. The woman, wearing a loose gown, holds a carding instrument in her right hand and a distaff in her left hand. The man wears a buttoned doublet, and holds a distaff (minus the wool) in his right hand. Both the man's head and the implement in his left hand have been chiselled off[12]. This carving is a celebration of life in the 15th century – an illustration of two hardworking folk, earning an honest living. This is also a reference to one of the local trades – wool and the production of cloth. The left and right supporters are a single leaf of foliage, representing the goodness of God's creation.

▲

The centrepiece features a mermaid and merman. The mermaid is combing her hair and holds a broken mirror in her right hand: these signify earthly vanity. The merman holds a stone in his right hand. Mermaids were a sign of danger and represent female seduction of men who are being enticed onto the rock of sin[16]. The man here has clearly succumbed to the dangers represented by the mermaid. The right and left supporters are single leaves of foliage representing the goodness of God-given nature.

◀

The centrepiece is an eagle rescuing a swaddled infant in a cloth sling. The eagle is the king of the birds, revered, symbolic of Christ and the resurrection. It is reputed to be the only bird able to look directly into the sun, as Christ can gaze upon God[13]. The eagle is rescuing the swaddled baby (representing mankind) from the clutches of evil. Both the head of the child and that of the eagle have been defaced in this carving. The right supporter is a half-man half-lion, which is representative of justice. The left supporter is a lion coward *sejant*, (in heraldic terms this is a lion sitting on his haunches with its forepaws on the ground[14], symbolic of cowardice[15]).

The centrepiece is a naked woman riding on a stag. The stag represents the wisdom and purity of Christ and the enemy of Satan. There are ears of corn to the left and right of the woman and there is also a flowering rose on the right side of her, symbolising the Virgin Mary.

Her free-flowing loose hair is not tucked away respectably under a hat, which in 15th-century parlance made her a "loose woman".

Despite being surrounded by all the beauty of God's harvest and creation (depicted by the ears of corn, flowering rose and the foliage on the left and right supporters), she is rejecting Christianity by defiling the stag and riding astride it. Her left hand is clenched into a fist against a scroll which symbolises the scriptures or the bible. Her right hand and arm are held across the flowering rose, symbolically blocking and rejecting the purity and goodness of the Virgin Mary. This is a very potent warning to men to be aware of, and reject, Satan's evil influence through lecherous women.

04

The centrepiece is a camel with palm leaves in the background. A camel does not need to drink for long periods and therefore represents temperance[17]. The palm tree and its leaves denote righteousness and resurrection[18]. The left and right supporters depict on each side a horned wyvern, a sign of valour, strength and protection.

05

▼

By complete contrast to misericord 4, this carving rejoices in God's divine creation of nature. The centrepiece is a double row of vine leaves arranged round a cluster of grapes with the left and right supporters showing similar leaf arrangements.

The vine leaves and grapes here represent Christ "I am the Vine" (John: Chapter 15, verse 5[19]) and the left and right supporters display the creation of nature by God. This is a celebration of Jesus, Christianity and all that is good.

06

▼

07

The centrepiece carving is defaced but the outline suggests a tumbler, with the left and right supporters depicting hanging masks. Tumblers, jugglers, dancers and grimacers were present at every fair and festival[22] and an extremely popular part of 15th century life.

This may be a warning that the devil lurks in all aspects of life, including everyday forms of entertainment, poised to snatch unsuspecting souls.

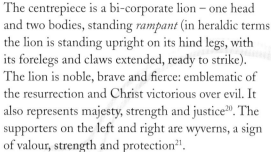

The centrepiece is a bi-corporate lion – one head and two bodies, standing *rampant* (in heraldic terms the lion is standing upright on its hind legs, with its forelegs and claws extended, ready to strike). The lion is noble, brave and fierce: emblematic of the resurrection and Christ victorious over evil. It also represents majesty, strength and justice[20]. The supporters on the left and right are wyverns, a sign of valour, strength and protection[21].

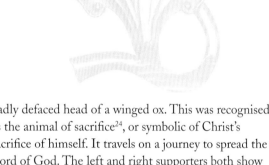

The centrepiece appears to be a coracle, a small rounded wickerwork boat made watertight using materials such as animal hides or canvases. The boat symbolises the soul "a coracle on a dangerous sea, oarless, until apprehended by Grace[23]". The coracle contains the badly defaced head of a winged ox. This was recognised as the animal of sacrifice[24], or symbolic of Christ's sacrifice of himself. It travels on a journey to spread the word of God. The left and right supporters both show foliage symbolising God's creation of nature.

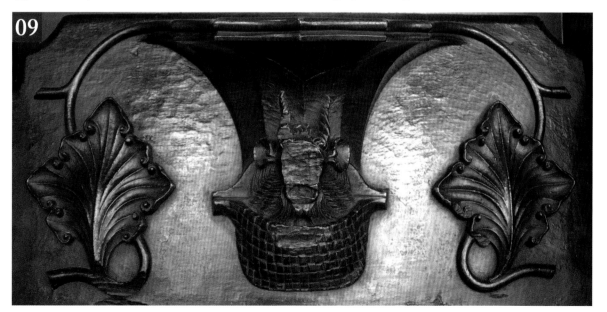

09

▶

The centrepiece is an owl, with its wings fully displayed. The owl is a bird that lives in the dark and symbolises those people who refuse to reject the darkness and come into the light of Christianity[25]. The left and right supporters both show foliage, depicting God's creation of nature.

▼

The centrepiece is a rose, with leaves, and a small shield imposed upon it. The left and right supporters are Tudor roses. The rose has various meanings. It is usually a symbol of Mary, mother of Jesus and therefore also the epitome of motherhood and purity. A rose with leaves is also a symbol of protection, because of the thorns. Alternatively, in heraldic terms it was also used as a royal emblem in the reigns of Henry IV and V, and hence has links with the monarchy. The rose is a symbol of providence, love, beauty, purity and passion[26].

The centrepiece, together with the left and right supporters displays the miracle of nature in three pieces of foliage, but of a different style from the vine leaves in misericord 6. Again, this is a celebration of God's creation and love.

Wall-mounted misericords

Misericord A *(wall-mounted on the north side of the chancel)*

The centrepiece is a mermaid holding a mirror and comb, both signs of earthly vanity. As explained in misericord 3, mermaids were a sign of danger and could entice men towards the rock of sin[28]. The right and left supporters are both leaves of foliage, a sign of God's creation of nature.

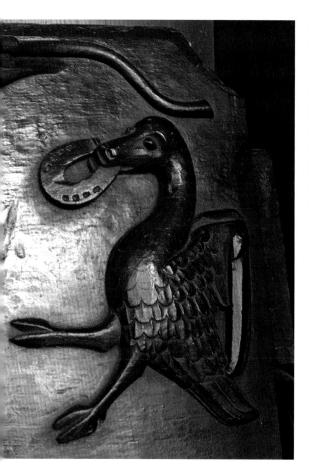

The centrepiece is a bearded man's head with eastern head-dress. This man is representative of the people of all those races not yet converted to Christianity. The supporter on the left is a duck, symbolising honesty, fidelity and simplicity. The supporter on the right is an ostrich denoting willing obedience and also symbolising meditation, holding a horseshoe in its beak to ward off the devil[27]. These left and right supporters together are emblematic of some of the main tenets of Christianity.

Misericord B *(wall-mounted on the south side of the chancel)*

The centrepiece is a bearded man, in 15th-century clothes, sowing seeds. He represents the month of March and this carving celebrates the miracle of God's new growth each spring. The left and right supporters are of leaves of foliage and also celebrate God's creation of nature.

South side misericords

The first misericord after the priest's door

▶

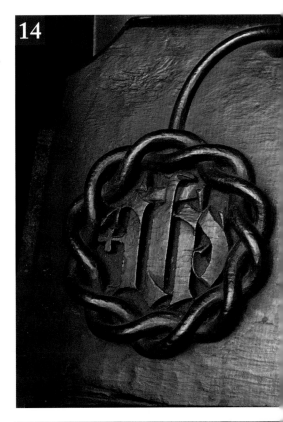

The centrepiece on this carving is a woman attacking a man. She is clearly very angry, has grabbed the man's beard and is raising a saucepan to beat him, while also trying to kick his shin. He looks scared and is raising a hand as if he is trying to protect himself while begging for mercy. There is no doubt she has the upper hand and the man is completely dominated by her. This represents the social order of life in the 15th century turned on its head, in that it was men who were expected to control society, not their wives. It depicts the result of a man neglecting his duty to discipline his wife and allowing her to take control. This domestic violence depicts the ultimate outcome of evil through the woman and lack of harmony within the home.

The left and right supporters symbolise the spiritual antidote to the violence shown in the centrepiece – following the teachings and love of Christ's peace, forgiveness and reconciliation. The initials IHS, are the first three letters of Jesus's name in Greek. In those days, these initials were used for the Cult of Jesus (a popular spiritual movement) to which many people belonged. Henry VII's mother, Margaret Beaufort, was a leading devotee[29].

▶

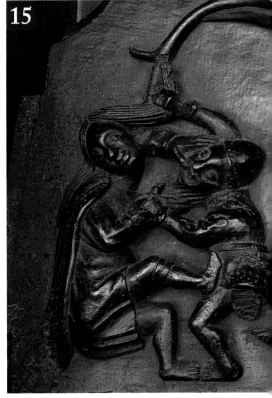

The centrepiece is a sphinx with rider (the face of the rider has been defaced). The heraldic symbolism of the sphinx is guardianship, divinity and providence[30], hence an emblem of Christianity. The left and right supporters show contrasting stories. The carving on the left supporter is a male and female fighting. The man has seized the woman's long loose hair (a sign of immorality), while she is trying to scratch his face. It seems that he is attempting to hit her but she is fighting back.

The man on the right has a grotesque figure (a naked half-woman half-animal) over his knee whom he is cruelly birching and his dog has seized her leg. Any animal with the face of a woman was symbolic of evil[31]. In those days men were allowed to beat their women, in order to keep them disciplined. The man on the right supporter seems to be highlighting where the man on the left has gone wrong. It is suggesting that the woman has not been sufficiently disciplined, and that the correct response would be to follow his example and beat her into submission. The dog, by his action, is supporting his master and joining in the punishment by seizing her leg.

▼

This is another centrepiece with foliage. The leaves are not the same as the two misericord carvings of foliage on the north side, so it can be assumed that as many varieties of leaves as possible were carved, to show the depth and breadth of God's creation. The left and right supporters are also leaves.

The centrepiece is two serpentine bodies, with their tails entwined; serpents were a sign of Satan. One has a monster's head and the other is that of a female. The association of evil with woman and the serpent dates back to the Garden of Eden[32]. The supporter on the left is a serpentine figure playing a pipe, again a connection between a serpent and ultimate evil. The right supporter is a man emerging from the mouth of a fish, holding its tail in one hand and a sword in the other. Fish, since ancient times, have been the symbol of Christianity. By holding the tail of the fish, the man is showing his allegiance to Christianity and the sword he holds in his right hand symbolises the power, truth, and strength of Christ in the fight against evil.

There is no centrepiece on this misericord, just three carvings of one woman; effectively it is a three-part story. She wears the same hat in each carving, the style fashionable for married women in the 15th century. On the left-hand carving she has her tongue hanging out, which is symbolic of the devil. In the middle carving her head is turned right to one side with an evil grin, suggesting that what she is saying and doing is socially unacceptable, perhaps nagging her husband, or spreading evil untruths or gossip. In the third and final carving on the right, she has been punished by having her tongue forcibly held down with a metal bar, in a "scold's bridle". This barbaric practice continued until the early 19th century[33].

18

19

▲

The centrepiece is a mask with a human face in the middle. The supporter on the right is a monster's head, surrounded by four large leaves forming a collar. A similar collar of leaves surrounds the human face on the left supporter. There seem to be two themes here. Firstly, the centrepiece strongly suggests a "green man", with the foliage spouting from the chin and framing the face. The green man is symbolic of God's gift of re-growth each Spring. The second theme suggests that man is also a part of God's creation and that, like foliage, humans grow and eventually die.

20

The centrepiece is of a human mask, with the horns of a ram. The left supporter is a dolphin *embowed* (in heraldic terms this means bent or curved like a bow). The dolphin was known as the king of fish and a specific symbol of Christ, guiding souls across the waters of death[35]. The animal depicted on the right supporter is a goat, a popular symbol of the damned, based on Christ's depiction of himself as a shepherd dividing his righteous sheep from the goats destined for hell[36].

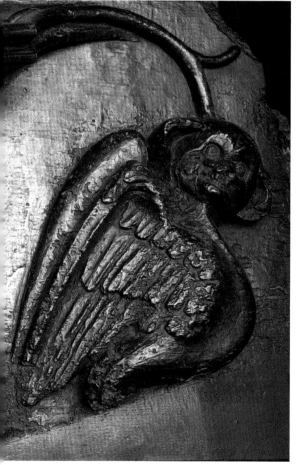

The centrepiece is a semi-nude woman, resting on her right arm. The woman is lecherous and dangerously evil. The right supporter is a harpy, a hag-like monstrous creature with wings, which was said to snatch people to tear them apart and terrorise whole areas[34]. The left supporter is another harpy which has been defaced. This whole misericord depicts lechery and evil.

22

The centrepiece is a satanic mask (defaced) with four horns. The left and right supporters both show theatrical masks. The mask on the left shows a man with a hooked nose, rather like a jester: the mask on the right displays a dignified, regal style of mask.

It was common for people to disguise themselves by wearing masks at fairs and festivals, behaving in ways which they would never dare to do in everyday life. Perhaps this was a warning to be aware of who, or what, was actually hiding behind the mask.

23

▲

The centrepiece has two upright bears *counter rampant* (in heraldic terms this is standing erect, ready for action) and muzzled, supporting a staff *ragulee* (in heraldic terms an emblem of pilgrimage and authority[37]) and they are chained. This is a slight variation of the badge of the Earl of Warwick, in his capacity as a local patron. The left and right supporters are monkeys (the head of the monkey on the left has been removed). The one on the right is producing a specimen of urine and the one on the left is examining the contents of a urine flask. Monkeys were regarded as similar to human beings but without any human restraints[38]; they were also a symbol of mimicry and buffoonery. These monkeys are actually taking a satirical swipe at members of the medical profession, as it had an obsession of always diagnosing illness from a urine sample.

◄

The centrepiece is a defaced St George, in armour, and the dragon. On the right of St George is a maiden kneeling in prayer, and on his left is a palm tree. St George here is overcoming the devil, symbolised by his slaying of the dragon. The maiden kneeling in prayer is the Virgin Mary. The palm tree denotes righteousness and resurrection. The supporter on the left is a grotesque figure, with the hindquarters of an animal, the feet and claws of a bird and a man's head arranging his beard. The portrayal of people combing their hair or men arranging their beards signified earthly vanity. Vanity was a deadly sin and therefore a representation of evil. The figure on the left has the appearance of a jester.

The centrepiece depicts the capture of the unicorn. There is a seated maiden with a unicorn's head on her lap and a hunter waiting to kill it. The small shield has three small crosses on it, symbolising the Holy Trinity. The unicorn symbolises Christ, who was born of the Virgin Mary and then crucified by man. The hunter in this carving stands poised to kill the unicorn and is representative of those who carried out the crucifixion. The left and right supporters both have carved oak leaves and acorns, symbolic of the tree of life and denoting worship[39]. The hunter's face has been chiselled away.

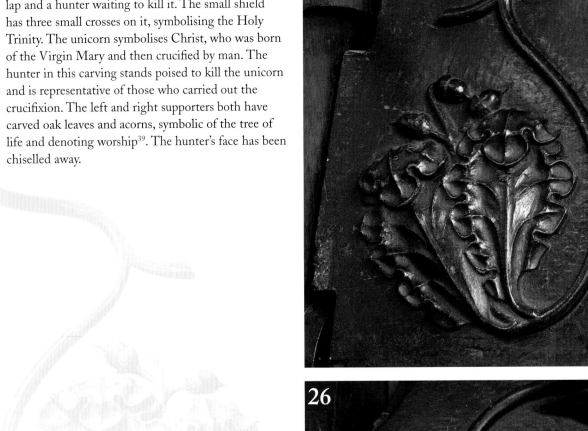

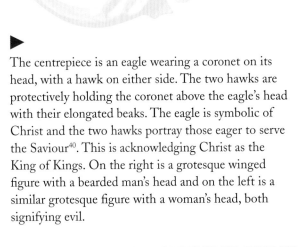

The centrepiece is an eagle wearing a coronet on its head, with a hawk on either side. The two hawks are protectively holding the coronet above the eagle's head with their elongated beaks. The eagle is symbolic of Christ and the two hawks portray those eager to serve the Saviour[40]. This is acknowledging Christ as the King of Kings. On the right is a grotesque winged figure with a bearded man's head and on the left is a similar grotesque figure with a woman's head, both signifying evil.

Bench ends

The nine bench ends are marked on the chancel floor plan (located on the inside front cover) with the letters (a)-(i).

Some of these bench ends were refurbished or replaced at the end of the 19th Century. There is no record of which bench ends have been replaced.

NORTH SIDE

Vine leaves and grapes

Leaves/foliage

Leaves (may be poppy leaves)

Leaves/foliage

SOUTH SIDE

Leaves/foliage (on Warden's seat)

Leaves/foliage (on Warden's seat)

Oak leaves and acorns

Oak leaves and acorns (the Tree of Life)

Vine leaves and grapes

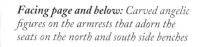

Facing page and below: *Carved angelic figures on the armrests that adorn the seats on the north and south side benches*

Notes and Bibliography

1 People who were infirm, elderly or unable to stand were able to sit on the stone seats around the edge of the church. The expression "the weak will go to the wall" comes from this custom.

2 Shakespeare's Church, a Parish for the World, written and edited by Val Horsler, with Rev. Martin Gorick and Dr Paul Edmondson, p 23. Third Millennium Publishing, London ISBN 978 1 90650733 6.

3 The Collegiate Church of England and Wales, Paul Jeffrey, 2004, p 10. Robert Hale Ltd. ISBN 0-7090-7412-3

4 Shakespeare's Church, otherwise the Collegiate Church of the Holy Trinity of Stratford-upon-Avon. An Architectural and Ecclesiastical History of the Fabric and its Ornaments, by J Harvey Bloom, MA, p129 London, T. Fisher Unwin, Paternoster Square, 1902.

5 http://collections.vam.ac.uk/item/0131750/misericord

6 http://content.yellowgrey.com/ms/a_handbook_of_medieval_misericords.php

7 http://bestiary.ca/intro.htm

8 http://content.yellowgrey.com/ms/a_handbook_of_medieval_misericords.php

9 BBC TV documentary programme, "Carved with Love: the Genius of British Woodwork", broadcast on BBC4 24/01/2013.

10 The World Upside-Down English Misericords, p 76, Christa Grossinger, Harvey Miller Publishers ISBN 1-872501-64-8

11 These two wall-mounted misericords were from the R.B. Wheler collection and presented by Miss Anne Wheler in 1865.

12 Fifteenth Century Misericords in the Collegiate Church of Holy Trinity, Stratford-upon-Avon, Mary Frances White. Published by the Vicar and Churchwardens, 1971.

13 Lecture VI: The Medieval Bestiaries from Early Christian symbolism in Great Britain and Ireland before the thirteenth century, by J. Romilly Allen. Whiting & Co. London 1887.

14 Fox-Davies (1909) p 184 A Complete Guide to Heraldry, London T.C. & E.C. Jack

15 http://www.heraldryclipart.com/symbolidm/l.html

16 BBC2 programme "Churches how to read them", Richard Taylor, broadcast 18/02/2011.

17 How to read a church, Richard Taylor, p186, Rider 2003, ISBN 184413053-3

18 http://www.heraldryclipart.com/symbolism/p.html

19 Although the reference given here is from the King James Bible, this text would have been well-known in the pre-Reformation bible.

20 http://bestiary.ca/beasts/beast78.htm

21 http://www.heraldryclipart.com/symbolism/w.html

22 Wooden Images, Misericords and Medieval England, Juanita Wood, p 99. ISBN 0-8386-3779-5

23 Quote from Bishop Francis Campbell Gray

24 www.catholicculture.org/culture/librarydictionary/index.cfm?id=37196 (From Fr. John Hardon's Modern Catholic Dictionary).

25 http://bestiary.ca/beats/beast245.htm

26 http://www.heraldryclipart.com/symbolism/r.html

27 http://www.heraldryclipart.com/symbolism/o.html

28 See footnote 16.

29 Information given by Martin Gorick, Vicar of Holy Trinity Church, Stratford-upon-Avon, 2001-2013.

30 http://www.heraldryclipart.com/symbolism/s.html

31 The Museum of Thanet's Archaeology, Kent http://www.thanetarch.co.uk/Virtual

32 The Museum of Thanet's Archaeology, Kent http://www.thanetarch.co.uk/Virtual

33 A scold's bridle used in a workhouse in Powys, in early 19th century, Powysland Museum, Wales. http://history.powys.org.uk/school11

34 http://mythmanhelp.tripod.com/id5/html

35 http://www.heraldryclipart.com/symbolism/d.html

36 http://www.heraldryclipart.com/symbolism/g.html

37 homepage.ntlworld.com/ksparnon/Ancestry_2html

38 How to Read a Church, Richard Taylor, p78. ISBN 978-1-846-04673-3

39 Church Misericords and Bench Ends, Richard Hayman, p 40-41, Shire Library, ISBN 978-0-74780-744-5

40 http://www.heraldryclipart.com/symbolism/f.html

OTHER PUBLICATIONS IN THE SERIES INCLUDE:

The Stained Glass of Holy Trinity Church – Stratford-upon-Avon   ISBN 978-0-9573142-0-7

In loving memory of Madeleine Hammond, who will always be remembered

Opposite page image: One of the 15th-century sedilia in the chancel
Opposite page inset image: Carving of praying hands created by Jim Dawes
Front cover image: Centrepiece from misericord 14
Front cover inset image: Tudor rose from misericord 11
Title page image: Mask from misericord 8
Back cover image: Holy Trinity church from the south bank of the river Avon
Back cover background image: Detail from bench end (i)